The

A SHELBY F. SQUIRREL ADVENTURE

The Great
FOREST
CAPER

ELEANOR LAWRIE

ACKNOWLEDGMENTS

Inspiration for this new Shelby F. Squirrel adventure came from Sandy Sakofsky's short story, 'STEPHEN', a brilliant tale of animals fighting back against the men and machines that threaten to destroy their homes. Written for adult reading, it is classic in presentation and execution. Thank you, Sandy, for allowing me to use your creativity as the foundation for The Great Forest Caper.

My heartfelt thanks to all who were willing to become beta readers. You each gave me valuable editorial and grammatical suggestions as well as generous encouragement.

Birgie Ludlow, thank you so much for working with me on the cover. Your artistic input and computer skills made it happen!

ISBN: 9798332499890

For Kira,
my beautiful daughter.

The SHELBY F SQUIRREL Series

As your child grows, so does Shelby!

BOOK 1
The Complete Adventures of
SHELBY F. SQUIRREL and Friends
Age 4-10 (Shelby is 3 months old to 2 years)

BOOK 2
The Great FOREST CAPER
Age 8-11 (Shelby is an adolescent)

BOOK 3
Where is Virginia?
Age 9-12 (Shelby, an adult, is now a father)

Visit Eleanor Lawrie at flutesandflyingsquirrels.com
Email: eleanorlawrie1@gmail.com

CONTENTS

PROLOGUE

Shelby F. Squirrel appeared in "The Complete Adventures of SHELBY F. SQUIRREL and Friends" at the age of three months, when young flying squirrels are taught to fly. Throughout that book's twenty-four stories, Shelby learned a lot about life and even began to grow up.

Now Shelby definitely isn't a little kid any more. He still lives in the same forest, with the farm right beside it.

Shelby, his sister Darby, and their mother are now part of one large family with Petra F. Squirrel, her brother Peter, and their mother. Petra and Shelby are constantly together, as are Peter and Darby. They love to play in the trees as much as ever, but are quickly becoming responsible, alert grown-ups. The mothers are content to keep the two large nests fresh and well-supplied with food, but all six of them continue to hunt together every night.

Ringtail and Lottie Raccoon and their children, Molly and Polly, have moved on with their lives, too. All four of them are the same size now, furry round animals with striped tails and saucy masks. Molly and Polly have found nests of their own close to their parents' tree.

Shelby's best friend, Marvin Field Mouse, still loves to spend long hours clinging to Shelby's back, soaring from tree to tree.

Rosie Robin has produced a new clutch of eggs every spring. These days the forest boasts several families of red-breasted robins who leave for the winter and return before the snow has quite melted, announcing their arrival by filling the air with their lovely trilling songs. Rusty, her mate, remains her faithful companion.

The Wise Old Owl is the respected leader of his growing family. Nobody in the forest questions his authority, and they all love him despite his gruffness.

The well-established friendships with many of the farm animals carry on as part of everyday life. Charlie is becoming elderly, but is sought out for advice, and loves a good laugh as much as ever. He introduces Shelby and his friends to his cousins, who have vital information.

Billy Goat and his lady companions, Nanny and Capra, are kept in the loop and Sultan the Rooster, with his extended harem of brown hens are frequently visited by the forest animals.

A family of skunks lives in the forest now, but so far everyone has avoided making contact with them, quite unable to face getting any closer to the rather offensive scent they carry.

Now something very frightening is happening in the forest. It will be necessary for everyone to join forces to try and prevent a major disaster.

1 MYSTERY IN THE FOREST

Shelby and Petra F. Squirrel were basking in the warmth of a beautiful spring afternoon, listening to Rosie Robin and her extended family send melodious notes echoing through the treetops.

Sunshine filtered through the fresh green leaves creating deep shadows against dancing rays of gold. Tiny motes floated in the bright columns, and butterflies painted flashes of orange and yellow as they flitted about. Shelby and Petra felt more like napping than gathering food. They would have to work a little harder to make up later, when everyone joined in the night hunt.

Shelby's sister, Darby, and Peter F. Squirrel, her new friend, had left earlier in the day, which was their habit lately. It would be nightfall before they would likely return. The mother flying squirrels were happily soaking up the sun too, high in the branches of the gentle pine where they were snacking on cones, digging out their sweet seeds, and finding clusters of soft new needles to line their nests.

Petra jumped suddenly, pricking up her ears.

"What's that noise?" she asked, peering around and then staring at Shelby with a spark of fear in her eyes.

"I don't hear anything!" he responded, trying to sound calm. He had seen a truck parked nearby a few times, and had an uncomfortable feeling about what it was doing there, but then he was naturally distrustful of new sounds and anything that might invade their treetop paradise.

"Let's go look!" shouted Petra, taking off into space with a flying leap. Shelby heaved a patient sigh and followed as she led him to the forest edge. Sure enough there was the small brown van, the same one that had been hanging around for a week or two.

They decided to follow the two men that climbed out and loaded up with notebooks and small cases, some on straps which were slung over their shoulders. One glanced upward, as though he sensed them above him, and quickly brought a camera up, snapping several shots.

"Couple of flying squirrels up there, Tony," he said, jerking his chin up.

"Yeah, hope we see lots of wildlife. Let's take a walk. You have your recorders all set up?"

"Yup, I'll pick up every possible sound from birdsong to mice running through dried leaves, you'll see!"

"Glad you're the one deciphering it later. I'll take care of the visual. Still shots on the way in and movie on the way back. Better if we split up, so I can record notes for myself. You wouldn't want my jabbering on your nature tapes!"

With a hearty chuckle he marched off toward the west boundary of the forest.

Shelby whispered to Petra, "Okay, you go with that one, and I'll follow the other guy. We better tell the Wise Old Owl about this tonight."

Petra had to stay alert to keep up with the photographer. He walked briskly, barely pausing to click the camera before swinging it away to forge ahead.

She began to realize he was seeking out the animals of the forest as he went. Their curious faces were peeking out of burrows, or around tree branches and between leaves. She spied Molly and Polly Raccoon clinging to the trunk of the tree where they lived, perfectly camouflaged in the dappled light and shadow.

Rosie Robin was easy to find while she continued warbling at the top of her voice. In fact Petra thought Rosie was following the man too.

Each time he paused to click the shutter Petra felt a kind of warm glow somewhere deep within her being. He was aiming at her friends and smiling to himself, quietly speaking as he did so.

But then she froze with embarrassed shock! He was looking directly at her, wearing a funny little grin.

"Well, well!" he said, as he aimed and snapped before Petra could react. He checked the result, laughing loudly. "Now, that has to be a first! Little flying squirrel wearing abject look of guilt! I do believe you are following me!"

Petra was horrified! She turned and fled, her heart beating frantically, crashing through the branches toward home.

Pausing to catch her breath on a sunny oak limb, her eyes widened as the truth hit her like a slap. Shelby wouldn't be home to help her decide what to do. He was following the other man! It occurred to her how much she depended on Shelby, a thought that came as a bit of a shock.

Totally annoyed with herself, she sat still to think for a moment or two. In the next split second, she was in flight, determined to finish the job she had been given.

It was easy to find the man with the camera again, but this time she scrupulously kept her distance. He was still taking what seemed like hundreds of pictures, sometimes bending very low and sometimes just clicking as he strode along. The whole time, his voice droned quietly, recording the details he would need to catalogue everything.

Petra began to relax and feel less afraid. He wasn't threatening any of her friends and he was being careful not to damage anything he came close to: a nest on the ground, the opening of a small animal's tunnel, or even the delicate blooms on blackberry bushes. She interpreted that as a deep respect for nature, and knew it was a good sign.

Meanwhile, Shelby was tracking the man with the fancy recording equipment. He watched him holding a big fuzzy shape with an outstretched arm, sometimes reaching high above his head, at other times bending low. This man was careful with his steps, proceeding quite silently through the grass and shrubbery. He was avoiding any dried twigs that would snap, and loose stones that might tumble or scrape under his boots.

Shelby sat back for a moment and cocked his head, wondering what this was all about. It seemed harmless, perfectly innocent. At least so far. Shelby's head buzzed with questions. Maybe a little visit to Charlie later on today would be a good idea, too, after they spoke to the Wise Old Owl.

It was early evening but the sun was nowhere near giving up for the day. Even though shadows were lengthening as Shelby and Petra floated across between the trees, they knew there would still be plenty of light. The two men had long since departed in their little brown van.

Suddenly the Wise Old Owl was coming toward them! He settled quickly as they hurried to meet him on a lofty oak branch. He folded his great wings and fluffed his feathers with a brisk ripple before speaking.

"We need to find out what those people were doing in our woods!" he said, with his usual tone of haughty authority. "I've never seen anything quite like what they were doing today, and I've been around forever!"

He had observed everything!

"Well," began Shelby hesitating a little, since he wasn't used to giving suggestions to the Wise Old Owl. He still remembered his own first night flight and the helpful lesson the huge bird had given him as a very young flying squirrel. Wise Old Owl had been a kindly uncle to Shelby and his friends for all of their young lives. They each had great respect for him and his extensive knowledge of so many things.

Straightening himself upright, Shelby said, "I thought maybe we should ask Charlie, if you think that's a good idea."

The owl's head snapped around to glare at Shelby. His eyes seemed to bore right through the tiny flying squirrel. Shelby flinched a little, and held his breath.

Finally the owl blinked once, and cleared his throat to say in his deep voice, "It's okay, Shelby! You're quite grown up enough to voice your own opinions, and I welcome that. Your idea to see Charlie is an excellent one. Let's go right now!" And as if on cue, another member of Wise Old Owl's family arrived with a graceful flap of his great wide wings.

"Howard, you take Petra and I'll take Shelby. Follow me!"

And with a flying squirrel clinging to each of their strong wide backs, the owls took off toward the farm.

2 CHARLIE

Charlie, the friendly old farm horse, was chewing complacently, one rear hoof tipped up as it often was when he was relaxing, long mane lifting gently in the breeze. He didn't move an inch when the two owls settled gracefully on the rail beside him. His jaw continued its steady rhythm as Shelby and Petra jumped off and scrambled over to face him from the other side of the manger, which was brimful with hay.

"Hi, Charlie! Sorry if we're interrupting your dinner!" Shelby exclaimed, his voice a little high-pitched from excitement and panic. "But this is really important, and we need to ask you something!"

As was his custom, Charlie's expression didn't change at all, while his eyes drifted from one to the other of his four visitors. As children, Shelby and his friends had often fidgeted impatiently waiting for the old horse to speak. They used to think he had fallen asleep at times! He was even slower now that he was older. Finally he swallowed with a huge gulp, and turned back to Shelby.

"Well, what are you waiting for? I can chew and listen, you know!" and he tossed his big head, laughing loudly with that familiar crazy whinny of his. Petra looked at Shelby and suppressed a giggle despite the gravity of the reason for their visit. The owls' eyes flashed a small twinkle, too, and then resumed their usual austere expression.

Charlie choked off his noisy private mirth, looking rather chagrined for once.

"Sorry about that! You want to tell me what this is all about?" Dear old Charlie loved to laugh and usually it was a most welcome sound, causing others to join in and feel good about nothing in particular. It was just Charlie's nature, although everyone remembered how the pigs had taken it the wrong way, and become offended, believing he was making fun of them. There had been a happy ending to that, with Shelby's help. Nowadays the wild neighing sounds made them wonder if Charlie was becoming a little senile. He was certainly elderly enough, with his gray muzzle, sagging back and jutting hip bones.

"That's okay, Charlie, but this is scaring us and we don't know what to do!" Petra explained sweetly, and diplomatically. Charlie just nodded and waited.

Shelby told him all about the brown van, the two men, their walk in the woods, and how he and Petra had followed them.

The Wise Old Owl sniffed indignantly, "Downright shocking, if you ask me!"

Everyone jumped when Rosie Robin came fluttering and almost landed in the hay. "Oh!" she panted, "Phew, let me catch my breath for a second."

In a moment she was ready. "I had to tell you! I stayed with those men until they got to the truck. They sat on a log together for quite a while and went through what they had done. I heard all the beautiful sounds of the woods, including my own singing I might add! And I could see their pictures; lots of them showed our friends in the forest!!"

Now that had everyone puzzled. What would be their reason for doing this?

Finally Charlie harrumphed softly and broke the heavy silence that had descended. "Okay, this is kind of good timing, but I know the farmer here is going to repair the paddock fence and I'll be staying where my cousins live, two farms over, while it's being done. Why don't you fly over sometime tomorrow? I'm leaving early in the morning, so it's lucky you found me here just now."

The next day dawned clear and chilly. Shelby was awake very early. He hadn't slept at all well. After rousing Petra, they stuffed a few morsels into their cheeks, and went to get Marvin.

Marvin F. Mouse was Shelby's very best friend. He loved to ride on Shelby's back and joked that his name should be Marvin Flying Mouse, instead of Marvin Field Mouse. But today all three of them would need the owls, who could fly anywhere and get there very quickly.

Marvin was waiting for them. "Hey, you two! Are we in for some fun today?"

"Well, not really, I'm afraid," answered Shelby, feeling like a bit of a wet blanket. "We have to go and see Charlie at his cousins' farm today."

"Cool! I'm ready any time you are," Marvin replied, bouncing on his toes.

"It's not a fun trip," Shelby warned as he turned for Marvin to climb aboard. "You'll soon know why, right now we have to get going."

They soared through the forest to the Wise Old Owl's huge tree where several of the imposing birds waited. Rosie and Rusty Robin along with quite a few of the family arrived as the owls were loading their passengers. It was typical of the robins to want to help as much as possible.

The air was still cool as they swooped down to light near Charlie. There were two other horses standing with him, their breath making little clouds as they swung their heads to welcome the motley crew of woodland creatures.

"Good morning, everyone!" smiled Charlie. "These are my cousins, Jacko and Goldie."

"Happy to meet you!" said Shelby, his companions endorsing that with smiles and nods all around. Rosie and her group arrived just in time to be included and then Charlie cleared his throat loudly. It took a few minutes of greetings and introductions before the business of the day was brought up.

When everyone was quiet, Charlie spoke, "Okay, You need to hear from Goldie. Where she used to live the horses were hired to take people for rides and they used a path through the woods."

Goldie was a gorgeous caramel-coloured

Palomino, with a lavishly long blonde mane and a tail to match that swished around her ankles when she stepped forward.

"We saw the same thing that you've told Charlie about, people with cameras and sound equipment. Then we found out they were making a film about how valuable all natural forest land is, and why it should be protected." She looked with concern at the small animals on the rail, and Shelby noticed that her eyelashes were the same creamy blonde as her mane and tail.

"So we're wondering if that's what's going on in your territory over there. They might be gathering material for a movie or maybe a book about your forest. We just aren't really sure why yet!" said Jacko, ending with a bit of a dejected look. He was a fine-looking animal, jet black, tall and sleek. His ears were uncommonly long which apparently had given him his name. Whether it was a reference to jackrabbits, or a hint to his possible ancestry, nobody knew or dared to ask.

"Hmm, interesting," mused Shelby. "That's better than wanting to do things like chase us away or change everything so we can't live there!"

Petra spoke up with an element of concern in her voice, "But how do we really know? How do we find out for sure?"

Rosie almost jumped off the fence in her eagerness to answer that. "We keep watching, all the time, and have meetings to tell each other what we're seeing."

Rusty bobbed his head emphatically. The

rest of the robins murmured things like, "Yes!",
"Absolutely!", "You bet!", and "Count me in!".

"Okay, okay!" Marvin exclaimed. "Super
idea, but let's be very organized while we go about
doing that! I think this is probably serious stuff,
and we need to be ready to fight for our homes if it
comes to that!" He was getting hot under the collar,
but sounding very wise. Known to be a happy-go-
lucky type, Marvin surprised everyone with this
impassioned speech.

After much discussion they agreed that
Marvin had the right idea. Charlie and his cousins
headed to the barn for the night and the owls
carried their small passengers back home, insisting
on dropping them off at their own nests. Rosie said
she would start first thing in the morning letting
everyone else know what was happening.

It was time to start developing a plan.

3 SIGNS OF INVASION

It had rained all night, with brilliant flashes of lightning followed by crashes of thunder that rolled and growled and rumbled on until dawn.

The whole forest was glistening in the morning sun. Everything looked brand spanking new, greens were lush, earth tones deep and pure. Wet black tree trunks etched sharp silhouettes against a backdrop of vivid glowing colours.

Shelby rubbed his eyes, and climbed to a higher limb to just have a quiet look around; he loved the calm after a storm. A rainbow curved high above the farm buildings in the misty sky, briefly spreading its dazzling glow of promise. Then he heard Sultan the Rooster crowing his announcement of the new day.

On his way to meet Marvin F. Mouse, Shelby shortened what began as a long, graceful arc to a lower branch across a clearing. He swooped and grabbed the side of a stout pine that overlooked the side road. Just a glimpse of colour that shouldn't have been there, but it was enough to make him want to investigate.

Peering around the trunk, he frowned at a large blue X on the rough bark. That had not been there the day before yesterday! Someone must have done this while they were at the farm talking to Charlie and his cousins.

Worse still, every tree in view was marked

the same way! Completely puzzled, he shook his head as if that would clear it and erase the ominous blue symbols.

There wasn't anything he could do just then so he turned back toward Marvin's nest.

His tiny friend was puttering about at the entrance to his burrow. He straightened up when Shelby arrived above his head.

"Hey, you're here early!" he shouted skyward. "What's up now?" Marvin could read his friend very well.

"I wish I knew! Come on, I need to show you something."

They went together to gaze at the puzzling blue crosses. Petra F. Squirrel joined them while Shelby and Marvin were still scratching their heads and looking confused. She almost shrieked when she saw the slashes of blue paint.

"What on earth? There must be a reason for them, there has to be!" she exclaimed, her eyes wide and real concern on her face. The only thing they could think of was to get to the Wise Old Owl as fast as possible.

Marvin hopped onto Shelby's back, "Let's go!"

The huge bird was fast asleep. His favourite time was always the dark of night, so he did a lot of sleeping during the day. Shelby and Petra did most of their hunting for food after sunset too, as all nocturnal creatures do, but they were still young enough to stay up and enjoy the sunshine. Shelby cleared his throat gently to try to wake their kind old friend. Soon those familiar bright eyes were glaring back at the waiting trio.

"Goodness me! Can't you let an old guy snooze at least a little?" he grumbled, ruffling all his feathers in a big shiver. "I was having a really fine dream too. You sure did ruin that!"

Shelby shifted from foot to foot and tried to be patient. Petra didn't manage to contain herself, though. "Oh, please, Mr. Owl!! Something is happening here in the forest. We found trees with horrible blue crosses on them just now. Someone must have done it yesterday while we were away!" she wailed. No time for diplomacy today. Tears ran freely down her plump squirrel cheeks.

The Wise Old Owl went stiffly upright, and said, "That doesn't sound good to me. I don't know what it means but the very thought is making me mad as a hornet! Messing up tree trunks with paint!! I never heard of such a thing, never!"

Rosie Robin joined them at this point, again slightly out of breath.

"My tree is marked with a big blue X!! What can that mean, does anyone know?" she said between big gasps for air. She looked terribly worried, totally upset.

The Wise Old Owl nodded sagely, then spread his huge wings. "Okay, I'll go and round up enough of my family to take all of us to see Charlie again. Wait right here. Back before you know it!" And off he flew.

Petra was putting up a heated opinion about

whether the trees might be marked for some kind of record keeping, and that there was nothing to worry about. Marvin was shaking his head so hard that Shelby thought he would make himself dizzy and fall over.

"Either way," Shelby interrupted, "we have to find out. It's our homes we're talking about! And the sooner we know more, the better!"

The Wise Old Owl arrived just then with two of his nephews, Howard and his younger brother, Hughie. They were subdued in the company of their esteemed uncle, but obviously eager to help. The owl taxis with their small four-legged passengers were quickly airborne.

Charlie was pacing slowly around the small enclosure on his cousins' farm. Jacko and Goldie were at the water trough. The owls landed on the rail near Charlie, their tiny passengers hopped off while the other horses ambled closer, friendly and a bit curious.

Jacko was the first to speak, "Here you are again, riding on owls. Neat way to travel, I would say!" He chuckled a little too loudly, obviously sharing Charlie's propensity for laughter. Goldie tried to ignore him, sensing that the general mood was serious.

Shelby spoke up to explain about the blue X's on the trees. As they listened, Goldie started nodding her head gently, and looked on the verge of tears.

"You know, don't you, Goldie? You've seen this before somewhere?" asked Charlie. He didn't miss much, even at his age.

Goldie couldn't find a way to voice what she knew. How does anyone tell a friend such devastating news? She blinked several times and released a long tremulous sigh. Finally Marvin F. Mouse started to squeak impatiently. "Heavens above! Tell us before we all keel over from holding our breath!"

Petra was chewing her lower lip unhappily, afraid to speak, choking back the urge to start sobbing in earnest.

"It's been a while," began Goldie, "but where I grew up there was a beautiful small wooded area beside our pasture...."

"So? What about it?" finally Shelby had waited long enough. "Please, just tell us, so we can get on with this!" He was immediately sorry for his unkind tone of voice. Everyone was on edge, but that was no excuse. "Sorry, I'm just so worried. That was totally uncalled for. Take as much time as you need, Goldie."

She looked a little hurt, but gathered herself and continued, "One morning, we noticed coloured marks on the trees. About two months later – oh, this is so hard to tell you. I wish I didn't have to!" She looked around with large sad eyes.

The Wise Old Owl spoke up at last, "It's okay, Goldie, you're among friends. Just finish the story. Whatever happened wasn't your fault!"

Goldie gave him a grateful nod, then blurted out with a catch in her voice, "They came and cut everything down! That whole forest was gone, and before we knew it the entire space was covered with roads and houses!! Then people moved in and nothing was the same ever again!"

A stunned silence hung in the air. An entire forest gone? It was too horrible to absorb.

The dejected little group thanked Goldie, said polite goodbyes to Charlie and Jacko, and left without another word. This would be a sleepless night for everyone.

4 PLANNING THE OFFENSIVE

Nothing happened the next day, and gradually Shelby felt his resolve return. He turned to Petra and said, "Let's do something about this instead of sitting here and moping!"

"But what?" she countered.

"The farm, I think. Let's ask Billy, Nanny and Capra, the three goats, if they have any thoughts, and I think Sultan would be a good source of ideas. That old rooster is super smart, and not afraid of anything!"

She nodded. Before going to the farm, though, they went to get Marvin F. Mouse, Molly and Polly Raccoon, and Darby and Peter F. Squirrel. Their mothers were busy relining their nests, which they did on a regular basis. Another chore for them involved keeping a stock of extra food in case of scarcity or bad weather.

Shelby and his little delegation of friends arrived at the chicken coop in the middle of the morning. Sultan was strutting about, checking that everything was in order, while the brown hens busily pecked in the grass for unsuspecting insects. They liked a juicy bug for a treat now and then to supplement the seeds and corn the farmer gave them.

Sultan turned to face Shelby and his friends, looking somewhat surprised.

"My goodness, I have a feeling you have

some important reason to come trooping along here in such large numbers!" he observed.

"You've sure got that right, Sultan," answered Petra, "we need to ask your advice."

The handsome rooster stretched his neck even straighter at that, taking it as a compliment. "I'm listening," he announced like a sober judge.

Shelby explained their worries, describing the camera man and recording engineer, and the blue marks on the trees. Then he told him what Goldie had said about seeing the same kind of thing and what had happened.

"We can't let the forest be cut!!" Sultan shouted, sounding almost as strident as his morning crowing. "We love having the forest beside our farm! It's so quiet and peaceful! And you would all lose your homes! Where would you go?" He was so immediately upset and concerned, hope soared in Shelby's heart. The others felt it too, a current of confidence. "There are ways to keep that from happening!" Sultan said fiercely, glancing from one to another.

"Really? Please tell us! Please! What can we do?" the forest animals all cried at once. Meanwhile the hens gathered around and obviously had been listening all along, because one of them spoke up.

"We can scare people away, we're pretty good at that. The swans would want to help too. People are very afraid of a grown swan on the attack, flapping his wings and hissing! The whole swan family can get involved, we'll make sure of that!"

"Right, so true!" agreed Sultan. "All we'll need is a signal and we can be at the forest in no time. I'm pretty scary if I crow nonstop while I flap my wings and run madly in circles!"

Rosie Robin arrived to join in, and chirped her approval while she settled on the chicken coop roof.

After agreeing on getting signals from the owls or robins, the hens and Sultan went back to scratching the ground with their strong claws, and pecking with their jerky head movements.

The next stop was the orchard where the three goats were grazing. As usual the grass was neatly cropped, with not a tall weed to be seen. They were very content with the job of trimming the orchard grass and lawns around the farmhouse. Nanny and Capra happily gave their thick creamy milk every day, grateful for the protected lives they enjoyed.

Billy, the largest of the three, had demonstrated his incredible head-butting strength the first time he had met the forest residents. Now they were asking him to use it again.

At first, however, the three goats weren't happy about creating problems for any humans. The farmer and his wife treated them with such kindness that the goats had a strong sense of loyalty. But when they heard all the details they came around quickly and agreed to organize themselves so at least one of them would come whenever needed. They assured Shelby and his friends that people always run from a goat that paws the ground and lowers his head!

Charlie was standing by the freshly built top rail of his paddock, smiling as he watched them approach. They all admired the new look, which made Charlie grin more widely, baring his long teeth.

Molly and Polly Raccoon climbed up a post and settled against the boards, Marvin perched beside Shelby and Petra on the edge of the water trough. Darby and Petra sat on the top edge a little further along. Rosie perched in the small tree in the corner.

"Well, well, half the forest population has come to see me!" Charlie said, still smiling happily. "So what's cooking now, my little forest friends? Any good ideas for doing something about this dilemma we're all facing?"

They told him about the goats and chickens being willing to help.

"Hey, I have another idea!!" Molly, one of the raccoon twins suddenly shouted. "We need to make friends with that skunk family that moved in last year!"

"Oh, no!" wailed Shelby, sounding the way he did at three months of age, so long ago. "I don't want to get sprayed by any skunks!! Phew, they stink something awful!"

Petra looked at him with disdain. "Shelby, I can't believe you said that. The skunks aren't afraid of us! They only spray if they're threatened! I say we go and speak to them right after supper before they start their night hunt for grubs."

Polly and Molly agreed, Rosie Robin did too. "That's powerful stuff, if we have it on our side," was her wise remark. Polly and Molly went home to tell their parents about the plans that were being put together.

Meanwhile Marvin F. Mouse, unusually quiet this morning, just looked from one to the other with a look of concentration on his face. Then he nodded, looking pleased as punch.

"I remember being told how afraid people are of mice! We're so small, but they just scream and run away. My grandma got into a house once, and when the lady saw her, she jumped on a chair and yelled her head off!"

"What?" Darby spoke up from where she sat with Peter, sounding quite stunned. "That's so silly! What on earth could you do to hurt a human?"

"We can't do a lot but we can bite, as long as we are careful to get away fast. We'll work on how to manage that, just a few of us. The others could make distractions to help us escape. I have a really large family, we have burrows all over the woods, I think a few of us can even build fresh ones nearer the forest edge to be close for when we're needed." The last part all came out in one breath, Marvin was so excited.

"Okay, Marvin, it's your job to organize your family and keep them up to date on what's happening," said Shelby. He knew things would be fine under Marvin's leadership. He was small, but he was determined, sometimes downright bossy.

Marvin nodded slowly, and said, "I'll get right on that. As soon as we get back today."

Charlie looked at the small group, and chuckled to himself.

"I'm impressed! You're really declaring war!" he said. "You know I'll be there to help, if one of you can just come and undo the bolt on the paddock gate."

"We'll do better than that, someone will come every morning to make sure it's going to open with a tiny nudge from you. But we'll leave it so it still looks locked in case the farmer decides to check." Shelby assured him.

Later that night the whole flying squirrel clan, Shelby, Petra, Darby, Peter and their mothers, discussed the plans, improving and perfecting as they went. First they reviewed the number of animals and birds involved.

"Okay, we have Sultan and the chickens, and they will tell the swans to be ready. They have to come all the way from their pond, but since they can fly that shouldn't matter too much," Petra said.

Darby said, "We could organize teams of watchers. Howard could fly over and bring the chickens and Sultan. And Rosie could get Billy, Nanny and Capra, because they're usually in the orchard, which is a bit closer." Nanny and Capra, Billy's two lady friends, also had horns, and knew how to use them.

Peter F. Squirrel added, "I'll help by setting up a nest at the edge of the woods. There's an abandoned woodpecker hole exactly where we could see the side road. Darby will keep me company, and we can take turns. Right?" he looked at her, but she was already nodding her consent.

"Okay then, Petra and I can do the same thing at the main road. We'll scout for a place first thing tomorrow," said Shelby, knowing Petra was more than willing to take on a bigger role in this venture.

Shelby's and Darby's mother wanted to help. "I can speak to Rosie and ask whether she can set up her family members to take turns on watch."

"And I'll visit Ringtail Raccoon and ask him to come with his mate, Lottie, on some days, and have Molly and Polly do it on others. I know they'll want to help. We all need to keep our homes safe," said Petra's and Peter's mother.

"As long as neither of you tries to come and help scare people away. Let us do the dangerous work. There could be trouble!" was Shelby's response to that. "We have enough on the action force without you. Just keep our homes here going, the way you always have, and that's the best thing in the world for all of us!" The other three young flying squirrels chorused their agreement, so the mothers nodded and seemed satisfied.

Peter reminded them that nobody had spoken to the skunks yet. "And I think the owls can take care of the rest of the warning system. We need to tell them what we've got so far and ask the Wise Old Owl and his family to set up their own duty roster."

It was almost dark, and the moon was rising against a star-studded indigo canopy. The whole family went quiet, thinking the same thing. This place was so exquisitely beautiful, with a vital community of friends, plenty to eat and wonderful neighbours who made life pleasant in every way.

Nothing could be allowed to destroy it. Nothing!

5 LINES ARE DRAWN

Shelby eventually volunteered to enlist the skunks. It took a little courage to approach them where they lived on the far side of the forest. But the meeting went very smoothly. There were two adults and four children. They lived in an old burrow that a badger had used before moving on to parts unknown. Actually they were all glad to help, being very concerned to hear of the impending threat to their home.

They discussed how they would be contacted when help was needed and Shelby returned home, a little relieved, because even in friendly mode the skunks gave off a strong repugnant odour.

"How did it go?" asked Petra. Both their mothers were looking on. "Did you escape safely?" She smiled coyly, waiting for his reaction.

"It was fine!" Shelby replied, "They're with us all the way, and it wasn't as bad as I thought to visit with them. I'm glad we can be friends instead of avoiding each other forever. I might even get used to that smell, you never know."

They spent the rest of the evening and their hunt that night stopping frequently to chat more about the plans and what could lie ahead. All six flying squirrels quietly took unpleasant thoughts to bed that night, rather than voicing how worried they were to each other.

And not one of them had a good sleep. They each dreamed about trees falling, animals running for safety, a strange place with hostile neighbours, losing track of each other and missing all their dear friends. It was the material of nightmares.

Early the next day, Petra and Shelby went over the plans again. They realized with dismay that they still hadn't found the time to enlist the Wise Old Owl and his large family. So after waiting until mid morning to let him have a little sleep, they swooped into the stately tree where he lived. Sure enough he was in owl dreamland, head tucked completely into one wing. They approached as quietly as they could and settled to wait on a nearby branch.

With a full-body shake of his feathers, the Wise Old Owl popped his head up and fixed his flinty eyes on them. "Here you are again! And you have questions, I assume. Lately you don't drop by just to say hello!" he accused, his voice rumbling.

"And we're really sorry to bother you, sir, honestly! But we've been busy getting some plans made for setting up our lines of defense," said Shelby, feeling quite guilty. He had learned so many lessons from this kind friend, he was ashamed to think he was only coming to him when he needed something. Shelby was unable to find the right words to continue.

Petra rescued him, "Mr Owl, we didn't mean to ignore you, but we've accomplished a lot, and need your help to make it all work properly. Rosie and Rusty Robin, with their family, will keep watch by staying near the entrances, but they can't cover all the small roads and the paths from the meadows and fields. It will take a lot more sentinels on duty, and that's why we're here."

"Never mind feeling badly, I like to get under your skin sometimes. Just teasing! Now ask away. It's wonderful to let the young people do the work for a change and make the decisions," said the Wise Old Owl, almost smiling at them.

Shelby brightened up right away, and hardly pausing for breath told him about all the help they had pulled together.

As their system was related to him, the Wise Old Owl stood straighter and taller, his head swiveling between Petra and Shelby, eyes seeming to open wider and wider.

"Admirable job! You will have all the help you need. My family does what I ask, and there are enough aunts, uncles and cousins to keep an eye on everything twenty-four hours a day, if need be!" he stated with a grand flourish of his right wing.

He promised to organize the patrols and coordinate the owls with the robins. They would also share the job of flying to alert the waiting troops.

Shelby and Petra thanked him profusely and went home feeling satisfied that they had done all they could to be ready. That final organizational job was the most important of all and the Wise Old Owl would do it with infinite care and expertise.

Each bird, whether it was a robin or an owl, would be the link to alert the waiting animals and call them to action. Not only did the birds have to act as lookouts and recognize danger, they had to remember who was on duty on any particular day.

They got home after sunset, and Marvin F. Mouse was waiting at the bottom of their nest tree. He had a small crowd of field mice with him. Shelby and Petra slid down the trunk to talk.

"My friends and family have a lot of very creative ideas for helping! Listen up, okay? We're going to make some new burrows near all the entrance roads. They won't be proper deep ones, just enough to hide in while we're needed there. That way we can be watching and be right where we have to be," Marvin told them. The other field mice all nodded and cheered and grinned at each other, clearly very eager to help.

Marvin waited for them to quiet down and carried on, "We've already got everyone set, so we know who has to be on deck and when and how long. We'll work in pairs, and maybe more when the burrows are big enough to hold us."

A slightly grizzled old mouse nudged Marvin and spoke up, "I just want to say that I've lived here a long, long time and I'll do everything I can, and I'm willing to die trying, but we have to save this forest!" He pumped a small bony fist in the air. That raised a loud cheer again.

Shelby thanked them, they all wished each other good night, as darkness began to descend around them. Another busy day, but so much had been achieved.

Quite an army was set to meet the enemy whenever that might be necessary.

6 THE FIRST SKIRMISH

Shelby's habit every day was to head straight for Charlie's paddock early in the morning to set the bolt on the gate so Charlie could push it open. He and Petra had discovered a large crack in the old oak near the main road, narrow but ample space for them on a temporary basis. And his sister, Darby, and her friend, Peter, were sheltering in the old woodpecker hole that faced the side road, as he had mentioned earlier.

Marvin had reported that there were now eight shallow burrows with room for as many as four mice in each. The farm goat, Billy, and his two female companions, Nanny and Capra, had come by so they would know their way around, and also how long it took to get there from the orchard.

Rosie Robin and her whole family were spread through half a dozen trees bordering the forest. She had forgotten to tell Shelby how skilled they all were at dive-bombing an enemy target, so she flew to look for him, and found him on the way back from Charlie.

"Shelby! Good morning!" she chirped merrily, "It's another beautiful day!"

"Oh, hi Rosie!" he was pleased to see her. She was always so cheerful, it was infectious.

"I need to let you know something, so you

won't be shocked, and let the others know too, please," she went on.

"Know what?" he asked, wondering what she was referring to.

"We robins are expert dive-bombers, anyone we aim for goes running, believe me!" she said proudly, despite herself. She was not inclined to brag, but facts are facts. This was worth a little boasting.

"Oh, that's amazing! Wow, yes, that would be super scary!!" he nodded happily, quite impressed. "Boy, if a flying squirrel floated by right after that, just when they think the coast is clear...."

"As long as we don't collide, Shelby," she warned. "We don't want any accidents, doing all this."

"I'll spread the word, and you do the same. It'll be fine, I'm sure," Shelby assured her.

The first warning to deploy the troops took them all by surprise. It rained for two solid days, and on the third, a   pickup truck suddenly braked and pulled in from the side road. Two men hopped out and busied themselves at the back of the truck.

Rosie's cousin, Merry Robin, started squawking loudly and dive-bombed the two surprised fellows, making them duck, then run with their arms over their heads and jump back into the cab of the truck, where they stared wide-eyed through the windows. One hurriedly put a cell phone to his ear.

Merry Robin took off to do her alerts and Howard Owl took over. Spreading his huge wings he swooped past the windshield, back and forth. The men ducked instinctively, even though he couldn't possibly reach them.

The one with the phone finished his call, and the two of them conferred, obviously arguing, and loudly. After a minute or two they climbed back out and, keeping their arms in the air to ward off Howard, started to unload their gear from the rear of the truck.

Howard watched from an oak limb, quite out of breath. He was relieved to hear crashing noises in the woods and soon Billy came through, head down.

He charged straight for the nearest of the two men, and knocked him clear off his feet. The guy bellowed as he fell, and came up fighting mad. Billy stood his ground and soon both men were back in the truck cab. Cursing loudly, the driver started it up with a roar and took off, tires spinning. Billy nodded happily at Howard and trotted off toward the farm.

Just before dark, the animals held a huddle in the orchard. Most of them were there to congratulate Billy, having already praised Merry Robin for her bravery. They thought things had gone well that morning, and everyone went home feeling very optimistic.

Life was normal for three days in a row, which let most of them catch up on chores and rest a little. Shelby spent the day with Petra, Marvin F. Mouse, and Molly and Polly Raccoon for a change. They enjoyed sitting in the sun, and made a nostalgic visit to the orchard to admire the pink blossoms. The apple crop promised to be a good one this year. Darby and Peter spent part of the afternoon with them too. It was wonderful to pass the time together, the way they always used to.

Molly said, "We don't have anything particular we can do to help save our forest right now, but we talked about it a bit. Mother remembered something from when we lived in the city."

Polly took up the narrative, "She said there was a real panic about something called rabies. One of our neighbours had been cornered and had bitten someone in his attempt to escape. After that things changed; traps were set, our relatives started disappearing! Rabies really scares people."

"So what we thought is we should try to bite someone, and start a rabies rumour!" said Molly.

"What do you think?" they asked in unison.

But Shelby was a bit shocked by this idea. He shook his head. "I don't think you should start biting people, no! That's getting too close as well. Do you remember anything else about rabies, besides biting people?"

Polly gave that some thought, then said, "Oh, yes, now I do, since you mention it. Mother said a raccoon with rabies might stagger, kind of walk a bit unevenly. That's perfect! We can certainly do that!"

Molly nodded eagerly, and added, "But we'll keep our distance. Just letting someone see us should do the trick. We'll keep out of sight for a few days after we try it, though. And let them think we've gone somewhere else."

"That's sensible," agreed Shelby. "We can't have you in extra danger because you want to help!"

They agreed to wait until what seemed like the right time, and then be very careful.

Later that week, Shelby and Petra went to see Charlie to check on him. He surprised them with a thought that hadn't occurred to either of them.

"You should have waited to see what those two men were there for," he stated bluntly. "For all you know, they came to the woods to do something good, and you've frightened them off for no reason!"

Shelby's heart sank. They had botched it! Oh, no!

But Charlie smiled instead.

"Don't be discouraged now, my little forest friends!" said Charlie to console them. "You just have to tell the watchers to hold back until they know that trees or animals are being threatened, then do exactly what you did! You know now it worked like a charm. Just keep doing it, but make sure the work rotation is fair so nobody works too hard, and keep polishing your system to be sure it always goes smoothly."

That made sense, and took away the fear of

failure already running around in Shelby's head.

He and Petra thanked Charlie, after promising to remember to keep opening his gate every day. The next morning was put to good use, meeting in small groups to update everyone with Charlie's advice.

7 DECEPTION

Several days of the comfortable peace and quiet that everyone was used to followed that tumultuous encounter with the two men in the pickup truck. Shelby mentioned it to Petra while they warmed themselves in the noonday sun.

"Boy, it's really hitting me today how beautiful our forest is, and how lucky we are to live here!" he began.

She nodded with a serious look. Their eyes roamed over the familiar view, with the variety of pine, oak and maple trees blending their shapes and colours. The robins were busy hunting for food; it was either morning or evening that their 'cheerio!' songs filled the air. Instead, all sorts of insect whirring, clicking and buzzing was reaching them on their perch. Two pale yellow butterflies floated by. Bees were darting among the blooms on the forest floor.

There was far too much to lose, and all these creatures would have to flee for their lives if the forest was gone. They had to fight for it!

"Oh, no! I hear something coming!" Shelby cried, pointing toward the road. It was the same pickup truck they had managed to chase away. He and Petra stayed very still, watching. They could see Marvin stick his head out of a burrow far below, and Howard Owl was sitting beside the

Wise Old Owl taking it all in. Then he quietly took flight. Shelby knew he was alerting the waiting skunks, just in case they were needed.

Their defense plans were very intricate, with a different team ready every day.

After a moment the men got out of the truck cab, one holding a cell phone to his ear. Petra whispered to Shelby, "They look nervous." Shelby agreed, and saw the Wise Old Owl nod, as if he was reading their minds.

The man put away the phone and opened the tailgate, then climbed up into the box. His partner waited, and took the two packs he was handed. They slung these over their shoulders and turned toward the trees.

This time everybody waited to see what the men would do.

With a jolt of horror, Shelby saw them each pull a can out and start spraying yellow streaks on the slender young trees that filled the spaces between the long-standing elders of the forest with their sad blue X's.

Marvin had followed with several of his relatives. They sprang into action like a well-practiced SWAT team. Each man suddenly had a mouse climbing up his boot as he stood doing his dirty work. It was easy to slip under the cuff of the jeans and sink sharp teeth into the hefty calf muscle above the men's socks.

With loud yelps, they started dancing and shaking the affected legs violently. Out popped a mouse from each waving limb, running madly for cover. But the damage was done!

"This place is spooked!" one of the guys shouted. "We gotta get outa here!!"

They trotted back toward the truck, the canvas supply bags flapping against their hips. Then with another holler, they suddenly stopped in their tracks, not knowing what to do. Their truck was ringed with skunks, tails high, their business ends facing outward. A pungent reek threatened to choke the two hapless workers where they stood, trapped. What they didn't know was that the leader of the skunk family had circled and was now behind them.

Quickly he turned, raised his tail and squirted with all his might, covering their pant legs in repulsive slimy guck. That got the men running helter-skelter toward the truck, where they were treated to further doses as they scrambled inside and slammed the doors. In a flash the motor roared to life and they were gone.

The skunks enjoyed a loud cheer from everyone. Then, understanding how their odour offended most nostrils, they wandered off for a well-deserved nap. Even if one of this family made an appearance in future, the strongest, bravest humans would flee to avoid the horror of being sprayed with that foul stuff!

Everybody felt a sense of accomplishment, but couldn't help wondering what they might face if the invaders became more clever.

All was well for the next two days, but there

was a current of tension crackling through the forest. At night the friends got together to go over their plans, they all trooped over to check with Charlie too. Some of them felt they couldn't measure up to the effectiveness of the skunks.

"But we need to keep doing something different, then it will always be unexpected!" said Shelby, "so don't worry, and stop comparing what you can or can't do."

"I agree, everyone has something important to contribute and it's the combination of those things that will make the difference." said Howard, sitting there beside his uncle, the Wise Old Owl, who nodded his solemn agreement. Their endorsement of Shelby's remarks was the last proof needed to believe the plans were good and they were on the right track.

Marvin was a little restless, listening. "That's all true! If we try to run up someone's pant leg too soon, they'll be ready for us. That would be a disaster! Just when they think they won't be bitten, we'll do it again!"

Molly and Polly Raccoon had joined them. "Now that we're on the list, we can't wait to try our act. We've been practicing walking all lop-sided. The only problem is we keep laughing at each other, so we have to learn to be serious about it," said Polly.

"I told you," Molly interrupted, "we won't be laughing when we are really needed, it will go just fine. I'll be way too scared to laugh!"

"I agree with you, Molly," said Rosie Robin.

"We're usually at a safe distance but you'll be right there on the ground. That would have to make anyone nervous."

"But you won't be alone, remember!" Charlie said firmly. "Our plans and schedules will ensure that. Every time the alarm is sounded, at least three teams are going to arrive."

"And we each know the order by now," added Petra, who had been listening intently. "We'll take them by surprise over and over, we have a lot of different acts to throw at them."

"We're learning as we go, and today we found out that it pays to wait and watch before going into action. The trees can hide us, so the team of the day can get there and be ready without being seen," Marvin said. Heads nodded all around the circle.

It was getting late, so the friends said good night and went home to their individual homes to try and get some sleep. The flying squirrels and raccoons were still up for a night hunt, so Shelby was glad the meeting was over.

"Oh, Petra," he said, when they were on their own later, "I sure hope all this works!"

"You have to stop worrying, Shelby! That won't help and a lot of us are looking to you for strength. So don't cave in now. We have to believe everything will be fine, and be willing to keep doing all we can to make that happen!"

"Can't you see how this is making our whole community closer? We can't just give up when we've come so far!" she said with such emotion that Shelby just bit his lip, and nodded.

They continued in silence, feeling the weight of the whole situation, and went home for a quick snooze before joining Darby and Peter to search for food.

8 ENTER TYRANNOSAURUS REX

Shelby and Petra were still dozing the next morning when they were rudely awakened, in fact it wasn't even fully daylight. With bleary eyes they peeked out of the crack in the oak tree.

The first noise had come from a large white truck, with a huge circular contraption on its roof. It was parked almost under their tree. The round saucer-shaped thing rotated slowly and then suddenly stopped as the two little squirrels watched, suddenly in full alert mode.

The other disturbance, which continued, was a sea of babbling voices as cameramen appeared and microphones were handed out, cables running everywhere.

"What do we do now?" Petra whispered, her voice shaky.

"Just calm down, they're not here to cut trees. But we do have to find out what they want, and the sooner the better!" answered Shelby, hoping she would not go into a complete panic. He asked her to stay and watch, meantime Marvin had popped out of his burrow not far away, and was taking it all in.

Overhead, the Wise Old Owl took off from where he had been perched listening. Shelby knew he was going to alert the animals who were on call today. Rosie Robin landed quickly on the branch, a little out of breath again. She was doing that too much lately. Shelby made a mental note to speak to her mate, Rusty, to suggest he keep an eye on her, and help her cope with all this stress. Rosie always tried harder then anyone.

"I've already got my people alerted and they're on the way. I told them to stay hidden for now, until we know what's happening!" Rosie panted, folding and refolding her wings nervously.

Shelby thanked her with a huge smile and she flew off again, this time to rest. Her job as sentinel was over for the day. There were enough others to launch a very effective defense line.

A few minutes later, Shelby could see a pair of swans from the farm approach and hide in the thick shrubbery. Across from them, a slight disturbance in the branches told him that Sultan Rooster, and a group of his hens were waiting patiently.

If they were here, then Billy or one of the lady goats would soon arrive as well. High in the branches, Shelby noticed both Molly and Polly Raccoon. They gave him a wave and resumed their vigil, ready to spring into action.

Soon Shelby's nose told him the skunks had also arrived, and were waiting nearby.

They were ready for almost anything, it seemed.

Finally, when the sun had almost risen above the treetops, they heard a roar in the distance. The racket grew steadily louder, and started to make the ground vibrate. TV cameras were aimed toward the approaching noise. The anchor woman, microphone in hand, craned her neck to get the first view.

Shelby gasped in terror when he saw a frightful monster, wobbling precariously atop a huge flat-bed truck. It was sitting on enormous tires with deep treads, and had a small cab encased in sleek glass. Sprouting upward ominously was a mighty crane that bent double and swooped back down toward the ground. At its end hung a massive set of jaws.

The tension in the air was palpable. Petra looked ready to faint.

The flat-bed truck parked and a ramp was lowered. The dreadful machine started up with a frightening roar and began to inch backwards..

Meanwhile, a smaller flat-bed had parked on the opposite side of the road and was unloading a miniature version of the leviathan that was now lumbering toward the trees. It chugged to a stop not far from the TV truck.

The drivers stood around talking, the news anchor woman was interviewing a man who appeared to be in charge. He was wearing a yellow hard hat, and carrying a clipboard.

The small machine was now unloaded and pulled up parallel to the larger one, literally dwarfed beside it. Shelby's head was spinning, trying to imagine how such small innocent animals could win any fight against those terrifying mechanical Tyrannosaurus Rex jaws.

All the excitement soon abated, however. The TV people packed up, stowing their cameras back into the truck, reappearing empty-handed, chatting quietly together. They locked the door, and got into a waiting car that had appeared without anybody noticing. Doors slammed and it was gone. The men who had driven the sinister machines down the ramps of the flat-beds climbed back inside their truck cabs, the motors puffed out black smoke, and they roared away leaving the gathered troops puzzled, relieved, and just a little disappointed.

Slowly the animals emerged into the open and gathered to talk things over. Charlie, the old horse, had arrived in the meantime. The first thing he said was how impressed he was to see the number of animals ready to launch a counter attack, and so quickly after the alarm was given. Their plans for being ready were working well. That was worth knowing.

Billy Goat spoke up eagerly, "We'll all be ready again in the morning!!"

Some of them chorused their agreement. But Molly and Polly were looking serious.

"We should see what we can do to break those two things they parked here!" said Polly vehemently, her eyes narrowed to slits. Heads turned to stare at her. Shelby was quiet, but he had been thinking something similar.

Molly continued, "We have pretty nimble fingers. We can try undoing anything that moves."

"We should see if those cabs are locked, and look inside for things to take apart," said Darby, who had arrived as the people were leaving. "Flying squirrels have pretty smart fingers too!"

"So do we!" added Howard, the Wise Old Owl's nephew. "Super strong, too. And our beaks can pull anything apart!"

They stayed together for a few more minutes before disbanding, deciding to meet later once it was dark enough to do some damage without being seen. The skunks had gone home so Shelby flew straight over to see them. This was definitely a time for their particular talent. They assured him they knew exactly what to do.

The moon was high when the chosen troops for the night's sortie crept silently out of the trees toward the Tyrannosaurus Rex monsters, where they sat gleaming dully in the night air.

The Wise Old Owl had cautioned everyone to leave the TV truck alone, explaining that it was only there to film or record the unfolding events.

"Word must have gotten out about what happened here with those two men who tried to paint yellow marks on the trees. That would explain the TV truck," he averred firmly. That was received with excitement, to think their plight and their heroic efforts would be made public. Perfect!!

Molly and Polly set to work on the tire valves. Howard found pulleys and springs to pop off, and opened the two gas tanks. Rosie and Rusty hovered nearby waiting. As soon as the caps were off they busied themselves flying to and fro, dropping bits of bark, dried leaves, and feathers down the malodorous black hole. Howard quickly screwed the lids back on when they had exhausted their arsenal.

Petra, Peter and Darby helped Shelby explore the cabs for things to undo. They twisted the knobs off all the levers. Marvin arrived with a horde of family members. Mice and squirrels chewed away together, industriously gnawing through every possible cable. Then they hopped down to clear the way for the skunk family.

Soon the whole area reeked, while the seats of both cabs were thoroughly coated with disgusting skunk slime.

They shouted cheers at each other, then they faded back into the trees.

The sentries went to their regular homes because they knew everyone was already on deck to appear in the morning.

9 AFTERMATH

Before splitting up and going home, the team who had wreaked havoc so brilliantly sat together near the ruined machines in a spirit of triumph and happy camaraderie. Even the skunks were included, and it was evident how much it meant to them. Tears glistened in their eyes now and then, but they were grinning like Cheshire Cats the whole time.

"Okay, now what?" Marvin F. Mouse asked brightly.

"Yeah, what if they fix everything and start cutting trees tomorrow?" said Petra nervously.

"Maybe they'll just bring new machines and everything we did will be for nothing!" whined Molly Raccoon. Polly nodded beside her as if she was worried about that too.

"Please, please! We have to stay optimistic, and believe in what we're doing!" Shelby pleaded, front paws punching the air. "Let's have a good sleep tonight, and come back early tomorrow to see what happens." He had to stop this negative thinking in its tracks. It wouldn't get them anywhere.

"And whatever that might be, we will figure out how to deal with it then!" finished the Wise Old Owl.

Realization dawned on all their faces: being united was the most important part, and that left no room for doubts or bad thoughts.

The father of the skunk clan spoke up, "We've never been included before, and we just want to say thanks! This will change our lives, I can feel it. The world feels like a pretty nice place to us right now! And we're so happy to help save this forest, it's a real honour!"

He was very well-spoken, which impressed everyone. And the conversation that followed was very enjoyable for all of them. Finally, though, it was time to get some rest.

They all slept soundly and peacefully, confident that their efforts would not be in vain.

When Shelby opened Charlie's gate in the morning, the old horse insisted on going to the forest right away to be there when the workers returned.

"This I have to see!" he gloated, "Never got to do anything this exciting in my whole life!!"

Shelby hopped onto his back and Charlie trotted over to settle behind the first couple of trees, well into the shadows. In the branches sat the flying squirrels, raccoons, Marvin Field Mouse and several of his family members. Each small mouse had been ferried up the trunk on someone's back. The robins sat high in the treetops on swaying feathery branches. More concealed, because of their size, were the owls, mottled gray plumage helping them to blend in.

Shelby noticed Sultan and half a dozen brown hens hunkered down silently among a cluster of raspberry bushes, and soon even Billy Goat could be seen peering around a young evergreen.

They didn't have to wait long; hearts started thumping when a minivan appeared and pulled in off the road. Two men got out of the front and several more piled out of the back.

"Holy smoke, what a stink!" the first one exclaimed. "Skunks, guys! Take a look around to make sure they've left!" They checked frantically in all directions, then continued forward with trepidation. When the foreman reached the side of the big tree-cutting machine, he let out a yell that brought all the rest at a run.

Holding their noses, or covering their faces with sleeves and handkerchiefs, they swarmed closer to the cab.

"Something's chewed the wires to shreds," one of them shouted, "and the knobs are all gone off the levers!"

"The seat's ruined, men, this is why we're smelling skunk here. Everything's covered in this horrible reeking goop!!"

Quickly, someone peeked into the smaller cab and confirmed that it was in the same appalling condition.

With great resolve, the foreman reached into the Tyrannosaurus Rex cab, inserted the ignition key and turned it. The massive machine started with a roar, then began to splutter. It gave several gasping heaves and died with a pathetic groaning shudder.

"Okay, that's it! This is outright war!" the foreman screamed. The other men backed off a little, not knowing how to react.

Just then the TV crew arrived in a small white car, and approached with curious looks on their faces. Awareness dawned in an instant and they dove into the parked truck, soon re-emerging with the requisite cameras, microphones and cables.

Everything was filmed, the unwilling workmen were interviewed briefly, and quickly retreated in their little bus, looking ready to explode with rage. The TV cameras continued to run, and a couple began focusing on the trees. Someone's sharp eye spotted the owls perched in a row, and then all eyes were straight up.

"Look at that!! There's a crowd of critters here just to watch! Something's really happening here. Man, will this ever be breaking news today! See how much you can get on film, people." All the rest of the TV crew turned to follow suit.

When one of them began to walk into the trees, and almost bumped into Charlie, with Billy right behind him, he screamed, "There's more here in the woods! It's like some crazy version of 'Animal Farm'!!" Then Charlie let loose a wild neigh and charged madly across the clearing and off into the woods.

The people froze in their tracks. That's when Billy Goat lowered his head and aimed for the cameraman closest to him.

Shelby screamed with all his might, "STOP

IT! These people aren't cutting trees, so leave them be. What they're doing could even help us!! Let them alone, and just go home quietly, everyone. P-L-E-A-S-E!!"

Billy swerved sharply at the last split second, his hooves throwing up clods of grass, and galloped out onto the road toward the farm, the cameras following him until he was out of sight. Sultan the Rooster and his small harem headed back into the trees, disappearing as quietly as they had come. Rosie Robin started singing to try and bring some sense of normalcy into this sudden craziness. "Cheerio! Cheerio!" she warbled, her eyes scanning as things settled down.

Molly and Polly Raccoon slithered down the tree and waddled off, and some of the mice got rides on the flying squirrels if they could, but the rest climbed down on their own and slipped into the burrows close by to be safe.

Shelby breathed a huge sigh of relief, just as the Wise Old Owl alighted beside him. "A close call!" he stated, "You shouted just in time, and good that you did! We need every ally in this whole venture."

"But what's going to happen now?" Shelby wondered. "It's getting more confusing all the time!"

"Don't worry, Shelby," his long-time mentor assured him. "I think things are developing just fine. And we still have our trees, don't we?"

"Yes, we do! Thanks for the reminder! I'll try to stay strong; I have to for the others, don't I?"

"It seems that way, they look up to you, and that can mean a lot. Puts a load of responsibility on you, but I have a feeling we're more than halfway there, and that this danger will soon go away."

Oh, how Shelby hoped that was true!!

By then the camera crews had departed in their small white car. But Tyrannosaurus Rex and his miniature partner remained in position, silent threats nobody was able to ignore.

10 WATERLOO

That night it rained heavily again, a steady downpour, and the pitter-patter drumming on the leaves became a sedative for the tired brains of the forest friends. Feeling happily well rested, they began to congregate at dawn and everyone was in place before any humans appeared. The air was crisp and clean, the morning so perfect it lifted spirits and built on the hope in their hearts.

The first to arrive were the work foreman and one other person. They resolutely inspected the damage together. A few minutes later, both straightened up after bending to scrutinize the insides of both cabs. One of them muttered, with a head shake, "No way that can be fixed quickly, and not out here at any rate. I'll get the flat-beds out again, and then we'll see what the garage says."

Several hearts beat a little faster. Shelby and Petra exchanged satisfied tiny smiles.

Then the TV crew arrived and set about getting ready to shoot. About the same time a familiar small brown van parked and out clambered the two men who had photographed and recorded in the forest not so long ago. They stood together, then approached the others. Petra's eyes widened into question marks and a small frown creased her forehead. Shelby nodded to himself, formulating his own thoughts.

Another half dozen vehicles had drawn up by then, and unloaded several individuals, some carrying shoulder cameras, others clutching clipboards. A few clutched small tape recorders; those were the newspaper reporters, each with a cameraman staying close, obviously working as a team. They started moving and fanning out.

More cars began to park up and down the road and little knots of people walked over.

Soon the two from the brown van took up a position together, with all the cameras aimed toward them. They spoke in turn answering questions, with mounting excitement, pointing repeatedly into the trees, then stepped back. The crowd was still growing, and Shelby realized most were there as onlookers.

Then the news people with microphones starting doing separate interviews. Photographers clicked in all directions and video cameras caught all the action.

Meanwhile the foreman and assistant stood to one side, looking very annoyed, frowning and grumbling to each other, occasionally pacing a little then returning to watch, clearly not wanting to be there at all.

Soon, inevitably, the horde of photographers and reporters converged on the two of them, filming all the damage on the two monster cutters, plus scrambling for comments from the men, who became more reluctant to cooperate by the second. There was an unmistakable swell of soft laughter and traded remarks among the cameramen and interviewers as they began to understand the truth about what had happened here.

A trace of skunk smell still lingered but wasn't deterring anyone from getting all the details of such an amazing story.

Finally, the still angry foreman and assistant were able to make their escape. The clearing came alive with boisterous chatter, shaking heads and even a few fists. Several got into heated discussions before they gradually dispersed and departed.

When the last car had disappeared, the animals were too shocked to speak. "I'm not sure what to think!" said Shelby. A soft groan went through the whole group, which he thought meant they agreed with him. Then the Wise Old Owl spoke.

"Well, I would say it's pretty obvious that those humans were arguing about the future of this forest. We have the photographer and his sound engineer firmly in our camp. To me that's quite clear," he said, nodding his head a few times.

"So, how are we going to know?" Shelby asked.

"We wait again, and see what happens next. Tonight everything we saw being documented by those news folks will be plastered over this whole area, into the cities and towns and far beyond."

Even though that made sense, when they took a vote the majority wanted to continue to keep watch and carry on with their response teams, have them available.

And even the Wise Old Owl agreed it was better to be safe than sorry. And it would prove to be a smart decision very soon.

Petra couldn't believe her eyes! She and Shelby were wakened by a small truck turning in and parking at the edge of the trees. There wasn't much space left with the TV truck and Tyrannosaurus Rex and his little Bobcat buddy still sitting there. When the driver and passengers alighted and dug out large chainsaws from the truck beds, Petra waved frantically at Rosie Robin who took off in a flurry of feathers. Howard was on duty too, and also flew quickly away. The men began to enter the forest, noisily pushing through the dense undergrowth.

Almost as if on cue, three saws were started up. With their motors burbling and belching fumes they soon had half a dozen small trees felled, and the men systematically moved forward.

Suddenly the leader roared and toppled straight backward, the saw kicking and bucking in his hands. And there stood Billy Goat, pawing the ground like an enraged bull. He charged again and knocked the second man flying.

The third one started retreating hastily, waving his arms in the air like a crazed windmill, dropping the saw which stalled as it hit the ground. An owl flapped wildly past his face, crying a spooky "Hoooo". In its wake criss-crossed Shelby and Petra.

The first two men had scrambled to their

feet and turned to run, only to face Sultan and both adult swans in a frenzy of flapping wings, hissing and crowing. That's when Molly and Polly Raccoon paraded through, looking exactly like inebriated sailors who hadn't gained their land legs after being at sea. As the men bent to pick up the saws, Rosie, Rusty and half a dozen other robins dive-bombed their upturned rear ends from every direction. They slapped at the birds, and yelled madly.

Shelby had stopped for a quick turnaround when he saw the cameras and announcers circling the scene with rapid-fire commentary, and wide lens coverage of everything that was going on.

Charlie had also arrived and issued a whinny that sent chills up Shelby's spine, while he raised his front legs high off the ground, snorting, and wild-eyed. Then Billy charged through again, followed by both Nanny and Capra. The men were frozen to the spot, stupefied. Then they lurched into fantastic dance moves, jiggling one leg, then the other. Field mice escaped in every direction but their sharp teeth had left patterns on the hairy legs under those denim pants.

All three men were screaming like banshees by then, and running panic-stricken for their truck. The saws were abandoned on the ground, mercifully stalled so they weren't a danger to anyone.

And every moment of all this was being recorded right before their eyes! It hit Shelby like a shock wave when he realized that a couple of the cameras were now concentrating on the upper branches, where all the rest of the flying squirrels sat scrunched anxiously together. Molly and Polly had climbed up after their performance, their parents Ringtail and Lottie had arrived too, and all four were focused on the action below.

In the next tree a row of owls sat, looking like kings and queens viewing their jesters.

That's when the entire family of skunks paraded into the clearing, tails aloft.

The news people stood their ground, getting another minute on film, then turned as one body, tripping over each other, bumping into tree trunks, but realized when nothing happened that it was all a show. The skunks knew who was on their side, and calmly kept walking, now being filmed again, toward the trucks by the side of the road.

The three men hadn't recovered their wits enough to drive off, and were sitting in the truck goggle-eyed with chests heaving. Seeing the skunks appear they came alive as if someone had thrown a switch. The engines screeched into action, tires squealed, and gravel flew as they made their escape. The chainsaws lay forgotten on the ground.

Shelby caught the satisfied look of the adult skunks, and realized how cleverly they had planned that entrance. It was so perfect, like the icing on a birthday cake.

The animals had faced a potential Waterloo but now they watched together triumphantly as the enemy departed in defeat.

11 THE SLEEP OF THE JUST

That night was filled with joyful celebrations all through the forest. Charlie, the old horse, and the other farm critters stayed for hours and everyone cheered repeatedly while tales of the day were recounted. Silvery moonlight had crept up on them and heads were nodding.

Sultan the Rooster snapped them out of their drowsiness by leaping to his feet, declaring, "There's work to do in the morning!! I can't sit here falling asleep!! People are counting on me to wake them up tomorrow!!" And he bustled noisily off toward the farm, followed by the little bevy of brown hens. Soon the others followed, with the forest animals waving them into the darkness.

Shelby stretched and yawned. "Me too, we haven't done much hunting for food today and tonight isn't looking like it will be any better. Time to say good night; we can catch up tomorrow. We've been leaving it to our mothers far too often lately." Both of those ladies were long into dreamland, content to let their young offspring do the partying.

Nobody knew what the next days would bring, but now the tables had turned and no major harm had come to their beloved trees.

After that, so many days passed without further developments that they all started to wonder if it was truly over. Still they kept their nightly vigils and the teams were always ready for action. Keeping that system in place gave them peace of mind, and kept them busy.

Then, after a blissful week, the morning quiet was pierced by roaring truck motors when two flat-beds drew into the clearing off the main road. The men worked quietly, rigging up elaborate chains and winches. They hooked up the miniature tree cutter first and slowly towed it up the ramp. Once it was anchored, that truck took its leave, with a puff of blue smoke.

The other team heaved audible sighs and began the work of trying to move the Tyrannosaurus Rex monster. They unwound much heavier cables and attached them securely in several places. The huge winch screamed in protest but finally the giant creature creaked loudly and began to move.

By now almost every forest animal was watching from a safe distance. They trembled with excitement and a little fear. If that thing toppled they would have to make a run for it.

It shuddered and shook, the windlass started to give off a smell of hot oil, but inch by painful inch the horrid machine was pulled up the ramp into position. Then it was gone with crunching gears and whining motor.

The TV truck had left days ago, so before their unbelieving eyes the area stood empty at long last. Still it felt wrong to conclude that the danger was really over. It was part of their lives now to be on the alert.

Emerging into the sunlight that flooded the grassy open space, a lively discussion was soon underway among the forest friends.

"We should keep our watches going!" declared Marvin F. Mouse obstinately. He was so vocal, the others were beginning to look at him in a different light. There was more to that little guy than they had let themselves realize. He continued after a breath, "If they try something else we have to be ready!"

"I think so too," said the Wise Old Owl. "It's become a normal routine to be on duty, and we're managing to continue doing what's necessary to eat and stay healthy. It's too early to let down our guard!"

A couple of quiet groans escaped, but a little denial would be normal. The majority ruled and they separated, some to attend to chores and others to go home and sleep.

Their daily lives assumed an almost-forgotten normal pace for the next week. The watch crews kept up their schedules, nevertheless. Then the TV truck returned one bright sunny morning. Fast on its heels were several smaller vehicles. Shelby and Petra stared, newly frightened. Rosie Robin took off noisily from over their heads, as did Howard Owl with that familiar great whoosh of wings.

A few minutes later, Petra poked Shelby and said, "Listen! That's Charlie laughing!" And sure enough, Shelby could hear him from the road. They both held their breath, listening. What was going on?

Soon a familiar figure appeared and came through the parked vehicles. It was the farmer! His wife was with him, but most surprising of all, so were Charlie, Sultan Rooster, several hens, and both of the great white swans from the pond. Trooping along behind came the three goats, Billy, Nanny, and Capra, heads bobbing rhythmically as they walked. They formed a loose circle when they reached the forest edge.

Another large van arrived and half a dozen people alighted. They greeted the farmer and his wife with a lot of handshaking and back-patting, then they all arranged themselves in a line facing the edge of the trees.

Every eye was on the TV truck now. Someone had unfurled a large white screen that hung down, covering almost the whole side of the truck. The bottom edge of it was fastened down to make it smooth.

By now Molly and Polly Raccoon, the whole owl family, all the robins, Marvin Field Mouse with a large crowd of his kin, and the entire skunk clan sat in little knots viewing the scene.

Charlie caught Shelby's eye a moment later and nodded his head, signaling that the forest animals should come closer. Slowly they did just that. It had to be okay, with Charlie and all those other friends surrounded by people. Clearly it was safe and even obvious that joining in was expected of them. So that's what they did.

It was a large and very unusual group that sat blinking a little in the sunshine, while the farmer started to speak. Then the makeshift screen on the TV truck lit up, sound filled the air, and there was Shelby floating past the pine, then landing on the oak's trunk, with robin song creating a cloud of sweet notes in the background. Scene after scene followed, natural poses of every animal and bird in the forest. Hums of insects, the buzzing of bees and crickets chirping accompanied them.

Suddenly a chorus of horrified gasps went through the animal groups, shocked to see the Tyrannosaurus Rex and his little brother in all their menacing glory. Then the screen exploded with action: swooping owls, dive-bombing robins, wobbling raccoons, charging goats, berserk swans, chickens flapping, Sultan screaming and running in circles, men running haphazardly for cover, and the skunks with tails raised becoming the stars of the movie with their unique weaponry.

At last the screen was bare and silence returned. Shelby and Petra exchanged glances, their eyes huge, unblinking. The others tried to gather their wits, but an excited babble had arisen. Then Charlie raised his head, letting rip his trademark whinny. Silence reined after that warning!!

"Now," said the farmer, lifting an arm toward the circle of beasts around him, "you can clearly see that you've put on quite a show! This film has been shown all over the country! Nobody has ever seen anything like it!"

Two more people had joined him quietly. The first one picked up the microphone. "This is the most unique nature film we have ever produced and it's created a tide of protest. Many meetings have taken place in high places, and today we know without any doubt that this forest is no longer in danger!" Of course! It was the original two men that Shelby and Petra had followed all those weeks ago!

The rest of the amazing story was related by each of the other dignitaries in turn. As a result of that film going viral, many public presentations and long closed meetings, every nature conservancy group for miles around had risen up and pressed for action. The public had staged demonstrations in front of government buildings, and the rest was now history.

They were famous!! Exchanging glances of sheer wonder, the forest denizens reveled in their victory. Party mood took over, and it was long after midnight before the last of them headed home to finally sleep the well-earned sleep of the just.

EPILOGUE

Early next morning, Shelby hopped off the barnyard fence beside Sultan just as the rooster was about to open his mouth for his first duty wake-up crow of the day.

"Hey! What are you doing here before I even do my job, Shelby?" he asked.

"Sultan, I came to help!! Life is just too good to miss one little tiny moment!!" Shelby beamed up at the majestic bird.

So while Sultan sent his shrill calls echoing into the air, Shelby yelled at the top of his lungs, "Wake up, wake up! It's a new day, and we still have our forest!"

"I'll never get tired of saying that!" he enthused.

Sultan grinned at him, his head on a jaunty slant. "And I'll never get tired of hearing it!" he answered.

The two of them made a complete tour of the farm together, then went into the woods to rouse any sleepyheads they found. On this particular very, very special day, nobody minded being told to get up and get moving.

In fact, it was the easiest thing any of them had done in a long time.

Two weeks later a small truck parked beside

the main road, two men climbed out, and efficiently gathered tools, posts and a large shiny panel from the back.   Curious   eyes   were following every move.

Into the ground went the two stout wooden stakes, and soon the board was fastened securely, facing the road.

When the truck left, Shelby, Petra and Marvin, Molly, Polly and half a dozen others scurried around to stare up at it in wonder.

Across a background of towering tree trunks sailed Shelby F. Squirrel!! Emblazoned at the bottom of the picture were these letters:

FLYING SQUIRREL SANCTUARY

Printed in the USA
CPSIA information can be obtained
at www.ICGtesting.com
LVHW051950080924
790327LV00017B/365